Hope this brings you
many sweet dreams!
Love,
Aunt Andrea

Treasury of Stories

Originally Created by
BEATRIX POTTER

Stories Adapted by
Emily Thornton Calvo
Barbara Armstrong Schwartz
Cathy Ann Tell
Sylvia Root Tester

Cover Illustration
Anita C. Nelson

Book Illustrations
Dorothy Hraback
T.F. Marsh
Anita C. Nelson
Pat Schoonover
Sam Thiewes

PUBLICATIONS INTERNATIONAL, LTD.

Louis Weber, C.E.O.
Publications International, Ltd.
7373 North Cicero Avenue
Lincolnwood, Illinois 60646

Manufactured in the U.S.A.

8 7 6 5 4 3 2 1

ISBN: 0–7853–1112–2

Library of Congress Catalog Card Number: 94–69606

CONTENTS

THE TALE OF PETER RABBIT   •   5

THE TALE OF JEMIMA PUDDLE-DUCK   •   25

THE STORY OF MISS MOPPET   •   45

THE TALE OF SQUIRREL NUTKIN   •   65

THE TALE OF BENJAMIN BUNNY   •   85

THE TALE OF THE FLOPSY BUNNIES   •   105

THE TALE OF MRS. TIGGY-WINKLE   •   125

THE TALE OF MR. JEREMY FISHER   •   145

THE TALE OF PIGLING BLAND   •   165

The Tale of Ginger & Pickles • 185

The Tale of Samuel Whiskers • 205

The Tale of Mrs. Tittlemouse • 225

The Tale of the Pie & the Patty-Pan • 245

The Tailor of Gloucester • 265

The Tale of Mr. Tod • 285

The Tale of Johnny Town-Mouse • 305

The Tale of Timmy Tiptoes • 325

The Tale of Two Bad Mice • 345

The Tale of Tom Kitten • 365

THE TALE OF
PETER
RABBIT

Once there were four little bunnies named Flopsy, Mopsy, Cottontail, and Peter. They lived with their mother under a big fir tree.

One sunny morning, Mother Rabbit told her little bunnies, "You may go and play, but be sure to stay out of Mr. McGregor's garden. He does not like little rabbits and he will come chasing after you."

So Flopsy, Mopsy, and Cottontail each took a basket, hoping to find some sweet wild blackberries. And Peter thought he looked rather fine in his new blue jacket with the shiny brass buttons.

"Run along, now," said Mother Rabbit. "I am going to the baker's." And off she went to buy a loaf of brown bread and five cinnamon buns.

Flopsy, Mopsy, and Cottontail were good little bunnies. They always listened to their mother. They went down the lane to look for blackberries.

But Peter was a naughty rabbit. He ran down the lane, through the fields, and squeezed under the gate to Mr. McGregor's garden! He could hardly wait to nibble some crunchy radishes and carrots.

First, Peter ate some lettuce and green beans. Then he ate some radishes. The carrots were delicious, but the onions were too strong for his taste. When Peter's tummy began to ache he went to look for some parsley.

But at the end of a garden row Peter saw Mr. McGregor. The farmer was on his hands and knees, planting young cabbages. When Mr. McGregor saw Peter Rabbit, he jumped up, grabbed his rake, and chased after the scared little bunny.

"Stop, thief!" shouted Mr. McGregor.

Peter was very frightened. He ran through the garden looking for the gate. Where was it? Peter knew he was lost.

Poor Peter lost one shoe among the cabbages and the other in the potato patch. Without his shoes he could run much faster. He might have gotten away, but the shiny brass buttons on his new blue jacket tangled in a gooseberry net!

The only way Peter could get free was to wriggle out of his new blue jacket and leave it behind.

Peter shed big tears. He was sure he would never find his way home.

Peter had no time to feel sorry for himself. Mr. McGregor was not far behind. Hop! Jump! Peter rushed into a tool shed and jumped inside a watering can. It would have been a good place to hide, had it not been half-full of water.

Mr. McGregor was sure Peter was hiding in the shed. Quietly and carefully he began turning over flower pots, looking under each one for the naughty little rabbit.

"Kertychoo!" Peter sneezed. And Mr. McGregor was after him again.

Peter leaped out the window, upsetting three flower pots. Mr. McGregor tried to follow him, but the window was too small. And Mr. McGregor was tired of chasing the little rabbit. So he went back to his work in the garden.

Peter sat down to rest. He was shaking with fear and was out of breath. He did not know which way to go. He was also very damp from sitting inside that watering can.

After a while, he began to wander around, going hippity-hop, not very fast. He saw a door in the wall, but it was locked.

Just then, a little mouse scampered past him. Peter asked her the way to the gate, but she had a large pea in her mouth and could not answer. She only shook her head at him. Peter began to cry again.

Peter wandered across the garden to a fish pond. There, a white cat sat very still, staring at the goldfish swimming in the pond. Peter had been warned about cats; he decided not to ask her the way to the gate.

Peter became more and more confused. He went back toward the tool shed. Suddenly, close to him, he heard the noise of a hoe—*scritch, scratch, scratch, scritch.*

Peter hid underneath some bushes. Nothing happened. So he climbed into a wheelbarrow for a better look around. The first thing he saw was Mr. McGregor hoeing onions. He had his back to Peter.

There it was! Just across the garden, beyond Mr. McGregor, was the gate! Peter ran to the gate as fast as he could and slid underneath it to safety. Mr. McGregor could not catch him now!

Peter did not stop running until he reached his home beneath the big fir tree.

Mother Rabbit was busy cooking. Flopsy, Mopsy, and Cottontail were having a supper of bread, milk, and blackberries. Peter was too tired to eat. He flopped down on the soft sand floor and went to sleep.

Peter's mother tucked him into his bed and gave him a dose of camomile tea: "One tablespoonful to be taken at bedtime."

Mother Rabbit watched Peter sleep. She wondered where he had lost his little shoes and his new blue jacket with the shiny brass buttons.

Only Mr. McGregor knew where Peter's clothes were. He had hung them up like a scarecrow to frighten the blackbirds away from his garden.

THE TALE OF

JEMIMA

PUDDLE-DUCK

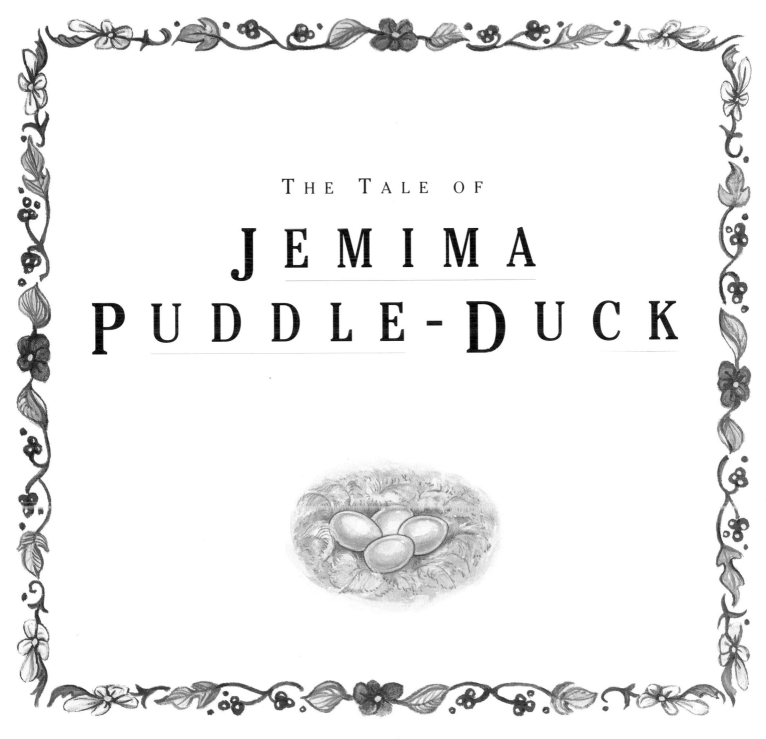

Jemima Puddle-Duck lived in a busy barnyard. She was unhappy because the farmer's wife would not let her hatch her own eggs. Jemima's sister, Rebecca, was perfectly happy to let someone else hatch her eggs.

"I don't have the patience to sit on a nest for twenty-eight days. And neither do you, Jemima," Rebecca told her. "You'd leave the nest and let the eggs get cold."

"I will hatch my own eggs!" Jemima Puddle-Duck quacked. And even though she tried to hide her eggs, they were always found. Jemima knew she would have to lay her eggs far from the farm.

One spring afternoon Jemima put on her shawl
and bonnet. She set off down the road that led over
the hill to the woods. She felt sure she would find a
safe nesting place there. When she reached the top of
the hill, Jemima saw the woods. She ran down the hill
flapping her wings and shawl. Then she jumped into
the air.

Jemima was not used to flying, but once she was up,
she flew beautifully. She skimmed over the woods
until she saw a clearing. Jemima landed and waddled
about in search of a dry nesting place.

Jemima was startled to see a handsomely dressed gentleman reading a newspaper. He had black, pointy ears, and long whiskers. He was sitting on his red, bushy tail.

"Quack?" said Jemima Puddle-Duck.

The gentleman looked up from his paper. "Madam, have you lost your way?" he asked.

Jemima thought the gentleman was very polite. She explained how she wished to find a dry nesting place to lay her eggs. The pointy-eared gentleman looked truly concerned.

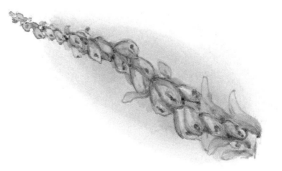

The gentleman folded his newspaper and put it in his pocket. "You may use my woodshed for as long as you like. Do not worry about a nest. I have a soft pile of warm feathers there. You could make your nest with them. You will not be in anyone's way, and you may stay as long as you like," he said. Jemima followed him to a gloomy little house made of sticks and mud. On top of the house were two broken pails, one on top of the other, which made a chimney of sorts.

"This is my summer home," said the gentleman. And sure enough, there was a woodshed behind the house. The woodshed was not in very good shape, either. It looked as if it was made out of old boxes.

When the gentleman opened the door, Jemima was surprised to see so many feathers! She did not wonder why they were there; she only thought how perfect they were for a nest. After she made her nest, she came out of the woodshed. The sandy-whiskered gentleman was sitting on a log reading the newspaper—at least he had it opened up. He seemed to be peeking over the top of it. The fine gentleman assured her that he would be proud to have a nest of eggs in his woodshed!

Jemima Puddle-Duck came to the woodshed every afternoon. She laid nine eggs in the nest. They were a greenish-white color and very large. The gentleman admired them all. He even counted them when Jemima was not there.

When it came time for Jemima to sit on the eggs, she told him, "I will bring a bag of corn with me so that I need never leave my nest until my eggs are hatched."

"Madam, do not trouble yourself," said the gentleman. "I will bring you oats everyday. But before you begin to sit, let's have a dinner party—just ourselves. You bring some herbs and two onions from the farm, and I will cook an omelette." Jemima did not think about this. She collected all the seasonings used when stuffing roast duck!

And when she waddled out of the farm kitchen, Kep, the collie, asked, "Where do you go everyday by yourself, Jemima Puddle-Duck?"

Jemima liked Kep. She told him the whole story. The wise collie listened and smiled. He asked about the clearing in the woods, and he asked where the woodshed could be found. When Jemima left him, Kep went in search of his friends, the two foxhound puppies.

Jemima Puddle-Duck waddled up the road for the last time. As Jemima began to fly to the bushy-tailed gentleman's house, she carried her heavy bag of herbs and onions with her.

As Jemima flew closer to the clearing, she saw the gentleman sitting on a log sniffing the air. When Jemima landed, she scared the foxy gentleman so much that he jumped. Quickly, he glanced about uneasily. "Come into the house as soon as you have checked on your eggs," he told Jemima. "Give me the herbs and onions for the omelette. Now!"

He said the words with such meanness. Jemima was surprised at the tone of the gentleman's voice. She had never heard him talk like this before. Jemima went to the woodshed to look at her eggs.

While she was inside, she heard the sound of pattering feet. Someone with a black nose sniffed under the door, and then locked it. Jemima was frightened. She did not know what was going on.

A moment later, she heard barking, growling, howling, squealing, and groaning! The whiskered gentleman was never seen again.

It was Kep who unlocked the door of the woodshed. Jemima Puddle-Duck was in tears. Kep had a torn ear and both puppies were limping. They helped Jemima carry her nine eggs home.

The farmer's wife let Jemima keep the eggs, but only four of them hatched. Jemima Puddle-Duck said it was because of her nerves. She was never the same since she met the foxy gentleman.

THE STORY OF
MISS
MOPPET

This is the story of Miss Moppet. Do you know why her eyes look so big? She thinks she has heard a mouse!

This is the mouse peeping out from behind the cupboard and making fun of Miss Moppet. He is not afraid of a kitten.

This is Miss Moppet jumping just a little too late. She misses the mouse and hits her own head. She thinks it is a very hard cupboard!

Meanwhile, the mouse watches Miss Moppet from the top of the cupboard.

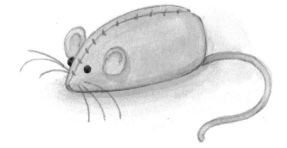

Miss Moppet ties her head up in a handkerchief and sits before the fire. The mouse thinks Miss Moppet is hurt. He comes sliding down the draperies to get a closer look.

Miss Moppet looks worse and worse. The mouse comes a little nearer.

Miss Moppet holds her poor head in her paws. Then she peeks at the mouse through a hole in the handkerchief. The mouse comes *very* close.

And then—all of a sudden—Miss Moppet pounces on the mouse! She catches him by his little tail.

Because the mouse has teased Miss Moppet, Miss Moppet thinks she will tease the mouse. That is not a nice thing to do.

Miss Moppet ties him up in the handkerchief and tosses it about like a ball.

But she has forgotten about that hole in the handkerchief. When she unties the handkerchief—there is no mouse!

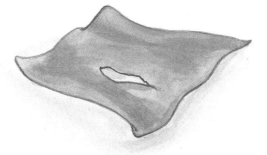

He has wriggled out and run away. Now he is dancing a jig on the top of the cupboard!

THE TALE OF

SQUIRREL
NUTKIN

This is a tale about a tail—a tail that belonged to a little red squirrel named Nutkin. Squirrel Nutkin had a brother called Twinkleberry. He had a great many cousins, too. They all lived in the woods at the edge of a lake.

In the middle of the lake was an island covered with trees and nut bushes. Among the trees stood a hollow oak tree. It was the house of an owl called Old Brown.

One autumn day, when the nuts were ripe and the leaves on the bushes were golden, Nutkin, Twinkleberry, and all the other squirrels went to the edge of the lake.

They made little rafts out of twigs, and they paddled over the water to Owl Island to gather nuts. Each squirrel had a little sack and a little oar; they spread their tails for sails.

They also took with them three fat mice as a present for Old Brown. The squirrels put the mice on his doorstep. Twinkleberry and the other little squirrels bowed and said politely, "Old Mr. Brown, may we please have permission to gather nuts on your island?"

But Nutkin's manners were very rude. He bounced up and down like a little red *cherry,* singing—

"Riddle me, riddle me, rot-tot-tote!
A little wee man, in a red red coat!
A staff in his hand, and a stone in his throat;
If you tell me this riddle, I'll give you a groat."

Now, Mr. Brown was not interested in a groat, which is a coin. He paid no attention to Nutkin; he shut his eyes and went to sleep. The squirrels left Mr. Brown and filled their sacks with nuts. They all sailed home in the evening.

The next morning the squirrels returned to the island with a fat mole for Old Brown. They laid it in the owl's doorway and asked, "Mr. Brown, may we gather more nuts?"

But Nutkin, who had no respect, began to tickle the sleeping Mr. Brown with a twig.

Mr. Brown woke up suddenly and carried the mole into his house. He shut the door in Nutkin's face. Soon a little thread of blue *smoke* from a wood fire came up from the top of the tree. Nutkin peeked through the keyhole and sang—

"A house full, a hole full!
And you cannot gather a bowl full!"

The squirrels gathered nuts from all over the island. But Nutkin gathered crab apples and sat on a stump watching the door of Old Brown.

On the third day the squirrels went fishing very early. They caught seven fat minnows for Old Brown and paddled over the lake to Owl Island.

Twinkleberry and six other squirrels each carried a minnow. But Nutkin, who did not have nice manners, brought no present at all. He ran in front, singing—

"The man in the wilderness said to me,
'How many strawberries grow in the sea?'
I answered him as I thought good—
'As many red herrings as grow in the wood.'"

But Mr. Brown was not interested in riddles—not even when the answer was given to him.

The squirrels filled their sacks with nuts. But Nutkin played a bowling game with crab apples and pinecones.

On the fourth day the squirrels went to Owl Island for the last time. They brought an *egg* as a good-bye present for Old Brown. But Nutkin ran in front laughing and shouting—

"Humpty Dumpty lies in the beck,
With a white counterpane round his neck,
Forty doctors and forty wrights,
Cannot put Humpty Dumpty to rights!"

Now Mr. Brown liked eggs. He opened one eye and shut it again. But he still did not speak.

Then Nutkin became very rude—

"Old Mr. B! Old Mr. B!
Hickamore, Hackamore, on the King's kitchen door;
All the King's horses, and all the King's men,
Couldn't drive Hickamore, Hackamore,
Off the King's kitchen door."

Nutkin danced about like a *sunbeam.* But still Old Brown said nothing at all.

Nutkin took a running jump right onto the head of Old Brown!

All at once there was a fluttering and a scuffling and a loud "Squeak!"

The other squirrels scampered away into the bushes. And when they came back very cautiously, peeking around the tree, there was Old Brown sitting on his doorstep. He sat quite still, with his eyes closed, as if nothing had happened.

But Nutkin was in his coat pocket!

This looks like the end of the story, but it isn't.

Old Brown carried Nutkin into his house, and held him up by the tail, intending to eat him. But Nutkin struggled so very hard that his tail broke in two. He dashed up the stairs and escaped out of the attic window!

And to this day, if you meet Squirrel Nutkin and ask him a riddle, he will throw sticks at you, stamp his feet, scold, and shout, *"Cuck-cuck-cuck-cur-r-r-cuck-k-k!"*

THE TALE OF

BENJAMIN
BUNNY

One morning, Benjamin Bunny sat in the sun by the side of the road. He pricked his ears to the *trit-trot, trit-trot* of a pony and cart. Mr. McGregor was driving the pony cart, and beside him sat Mrs. McGregor, wearing her best bonnet.

As soon as they had passed, Benjamin Bunny got an idea. With a hop, skip, and a jump, he set off to visit his cousins who lived in the woods behind Mr. McGregor's garden.

Benjamin's aunt, Old Mrs. Rabbit, made her living by knitting mittens and scarves. She also sold herbs, rosemary tea, and lavender.

But Benjamin had not come to visit his aunt. He was looking for his cousin Peter. He went around to the back of the fir tree and nearly stumbled over Peter. Peter was sitting by himself, and he didn't look too happy. He was dressed only in a red cotton handerkerchief, which he held tightly around him.

"Peter," whispered Benjamin, "where are your clothes?"

Peter told Benjamin how he had been chased through Mr. McGregor's garden and had lost his shoes and coat. Mr. McGregor was using them as a scarecrow in the vegetable garden.

Little Benjamin sat down beside his cousin. He told Peter that Mr. and Mrs. McGregor would probably be gone for the whole day because Mrs. McGregor was wearing her best bonnet. He told Peter they could go to Mr. McGregor's garden and rescue Peter's clothes. Peter did think a walk might do him good.

Peter and Benjamin climbed to the top of Mr. McGregor's garden wall. They looked down and saw Peter's coat and shoes hanging like a scarecrow. A knitted cap topped off the scarecrow's outfit.

Benjamin said, "We will get dirty if we squeeze under the gate. We should climb down the pear tree to get into the garden."

Peter fell into the garden head first. But he landed in a lettuce bed that was quite soft.

They took Peter's clothes off the scarecrow poles. It had rained during the night, and his shoes were filled with water. His little blue coat had shrunk, and the shiny brass buttons were all missing. Benjamin tried on the cap, but it was too big for him.

Now that Peter had his clothes again, they would be able to use the handkerchief for something else.

Benjamin began to fill the handkerchief with onions, as a present for Peter's mother. He felt perfectly at home here and ate a lettuce leaf. He said he often came to Mr. McGregor's garden with his father to get lettuce for their dinner. Mr. McGregor's lettuce was certainly very tasty.

Peter did not eat anything, though. He was not enjoying himself. He kept hearing noises. He wanted to go home.

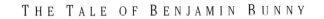

The little bunnies knew they would not be able to climb up the pear tree with their bundle of onions. Instead, they walked through the vegetables to the other end of the garden.

Soon they were among the flowerpots, baskets, and tools. Peter heard noises more than ever! Suddenly, he stopped. His eyes were as big as lollipops!

Benjamin took one look, and in no time, he and Peter had hidden themselves—and the onions—under a large basket. The two bunnies had seen a big barn cat napping in the afternoon sun!

The cat awoke and stretched. She walked to the upside-down basket and gave it a sniff. She sat right down on top of the basket! (She must have liked the smell of onions!) And there she sat—for *five hours.*

The sun was setting over the trees in the woods, but still the cat sat on top of the basket. Peter and Benjamin were trapped. It was quite dark, and the smell of onions was awful. Peter Rabbit and Benjamin Bunny began to cry.

Through their tears, the two bunnies heard a *pitter patter, pitter patter;* stones were falling from the garden wall. The cat looked up and saw Old Mr. Benjamin Bunny walking along the top of the wall. He was looking for his son.

Old Mr. Bunny was not afraid of cats at all. He jumped from the wall onto the cat and pushed her off the basket! Then he kicked her into the greenhouse, scratching off a bit of fur. The cat was too surprised to scratch back!

After Mr. Bunny had knocked the cat inside the greenhouse, he locked the door. He came right back to the basket and pulled Benjamin and Peter out by the ears. He picked up the bundle of onions and marched the two bad rabbits out of the garden. Old Mr. Bunny scolded them all the way home! He made sure Benjamin and Peter were sorry for their mischief.

When Mr. McGregor returned home, he saw several puzzling things. His scarecrow had been robbed of its shoes and jacket, and there were footprints all around it. The footprints were very, *very* small! Also, he could not understand how the cat could have shut herself up in the greenhouse—and locked the door from the outside!

Old Mrs. Rabbit was so glad to see Peter wearing his shoes and jacket, she quite forgot to scold him for wandering off. She was pleased with the bundle of onions, as well. She tied them up and hung them from the kitchen ceiling with her bunches of herbs and lavender.

THE TALE OF THE FLOPSY BUNNIES

When Benjamin Bunny grew up he married Flopsy, Peter Rabbit's sister. They had such a large family that everyone just called them the "Flopsy Bunnies."

Because there was not always enough to eat, Benjamin used to borrow cabbages from Peter Rabbit, who had a vegetable garden. But sometimes Peter Rabbit had no cabbages to spare. When this happened, the Flopsy Bunnies went across the field to a trash pile in the ditch outside Mr. McGregor's garden.

Mr. McGregor's trash pile was a jumble of jars and paper bags, oily-tasting grass clippings, rotten vegetables, and an old boot or two. One day—oh joy!—there was overgrown lettuce, which had gone to flower.

Benjamin and his Flopsy Bunny children stuffed themselves with the lettuce leaves. With their tummies full, the bunnies grew sleepy and lay down in the soft grass clippings. Before going to sleep, Benjamin slipped a paper bag over his head to keep the flies from bothering him.

The little Flopsy Bunnies slept soundly in the warm sun. From the lawn beyond the garden came the faraway hum of Mr. McGregor's lawn mower. The bluebottle flies buzzed about the wall, and a little old mouse named Thomasina Tittlemouse picked over the trash pile. She rustled across the paper bag and woke Benjamin Bunny.

While Thomasina and Benjamin were chatting, they heard the steps of heavy boots. Benjamin hid under his paper bag and Thomasina Tittlemouse crept inside a jar. Suddenly, Mr. McGregor emptied a sackful of grass clippings right on top of the sleeping Flopsy Bunnies!

The little bunnies smiled sweetly in their sleep. They did not wake up in the shower of grass. They dreamed their mother was tucking them into their beds.

Mr. McGregor looked down after emptying his sack. He saw the tips of some furry little ears sticking up through the grass clippings. He stared at the little ears for a long time.

Then a fly settled on one of the ears. And the ear twitched.

Mr. McGregor climbed down onto the trash pile. "One, two, three, four, five, six little rabbits for supper!" he said, as he put the sleeping bunnies into his sack. The Flopsy Bunnies dreamed their mother was turning them over in their beds. They still did not wake up.

Mr. McGregor tied the top of the sack with string and put it on the edge of the garden wall. He left the sack sitting there while he went to put away his lawn mower.

While he was gone, Mrs. Flopsy Bunny came across the field. She looked at the sack sitting on the garden wall. She wondered where Benjamin and her children were. While she was standing there trying to figure out what was going on, she heard a rustling noise off to the side. Thomasina Tittlemouse came out of her jar and Benjamin took the paper bag from his head. They told Flopsy the sad tale.

Benjamin and Flopsy were without hope. They looked at the sack where their sleeping bunnies lay helpless. Benjamin and Flopsy took the sack down, but could not untie the string that bound it. What could be done? They were afraid of what might happen if they could not come up with an idea soon.

Mrs. Tittlemouse was a very clever mouse. Thinking quickly, she began to nibble a hole in the bottom corner of the sack! The little bunnies were pulled out and awakened.

Benjamin and Flopsy then filled the sack with three rotten squashes, an old boot brush, and two overly ripe turnips. Then they all hid under a bush and watched for Mr. McGregor.

After a while, Mr. McGregor came back. He picked up the sack and carried it off. The Flopsy Bunnies followed at a safe distance. They watched him go into his house. They crept to the window to watch and listen.

The littlest Flopsy Bunny wanted to get a better look at what was happening, so he crawled up onto the windowsill.

Mr. McGregor pulled his chair from the table and sat down. The Flopsy Bunnies heard him chuckle, "One, two, three, four, five, six little rabbits!"

"Eh? What's that?" asked Mrs. McGregor. "What have the rabbits been spoiling now?"

Mr. McGregor only repeated, "One, two, three, four, five, six fat, little rabbits!"

"Don't be a silly old man," scolded Mrs. McGregor. "Tell me what you mean!"

"In the sack!" Mr. McGregor pointed to the lumpy sack on the table. "Six little rabbits for supper!"

Mrs. McGregor looked at the sack on the table.

Mrs. McGregor reached out to feel the sack. "They must be *old* rabbits. They are hard and are all different shapes." She untied the sack and reached inside.

When she found the rotten vegetables and old boot brush she grew angry. She was sure Mr. McGregor had tried to trick her. She did not like his idea of a joke one little bit!

Mr. McGregor was angry, too. He threw one of the squashes right out the kitchen window. He just missed hitting the youngest Flopsy Bunny!

Benjamin and Flopsy decided it was time to go home.

That Christmas, Thomasina Tittlemouse was given a very lovely gift. The grateful Flopsy Bunnies presented her with enough soft rabbit fur to make herself a coat, a hood, a handsome muff, and a pair of warm mittens.

THE TALE OF
MRS. TIGGY-WINKLE

Once upon a time there was a little girl named Lucie who lived on a farm. She was a good little girl, but she was always losing her pocket handkerchiefs!

One day little Lucie came into the farmyard crying, "I've lost my handkerchief! Three handkerchiefs and a pinafore! Have *you* seen them, Tabby Kitten?"

The kitten went on washing her white paws. Lucie asked a speckled hen, "Sally Henny-Penny, have you found three handkerchiefs?"

But the speckled hen ran into the barn clucking, "I go barefoot, barefoot, barefoot!"

Lucie climbed the steps in the garden wall and looked up at the hillside. She thought she saw some white things spread upon the grass.

Lucie scrambled up the hill as fast as her legs would carry her. She ran along a steep pathway—up and up. Soon she came to a spring bubbling up from the hillside. And where the sand upon the path was wet, there were footprints of a *very* small person.

The path ended under a big rock. There were clotheslines of braided grasses hanging from stems and sticks; a heap of tiny clothespins was on the ground. But there were no handkerchiefs!

There was something else, though—a door! It led straight into the hill, and beyond it someone was singing:

"Lily-white and clean, oh!
With little frills between, oh!
Smooth and hot—red rusty spot
Never here be seen, oh!"

Lucie's knock interrupted the song. A frightened little voice called out, "Who's there?"

Lucie opened the door and gazed upon a nice clean kitchen. It was just like any other farm kitchen, except that the ceiling was so low that Lucie's head nearly touched it. The pots and pans were small, and so was everything else.

There, at the table with an iron in her hand, stood a very short, plump person staring anxiously at Lucie. Her print gown was tucked up, and she was wearing a large apron over her striped petticoat. Her little black nose went *sniffle, snuffle,* and her eyes went *twinkle, twinkle.* And underneath her cap—where Lucie had yellow curls—the little person had PRICKLES!

"Who are you?" asked Lucie. "Have you seen my pocket handkerchiefs?"

The little person curtsied. "Oh, yes, miss. My name is Mrs. Tiggy-Winkle." And she took something out of a clothes basket, and spread it on the ironing blanket.

"That's not my handkerchief," said Lucie.

"Oh, no, if you please, miss, that's a little red vest belonging to Cock Robin!" And she ironed it and folded it. Mrs. Tiggy-Winkle took another hot iron from the fire.

"There's one of my handkerchiefs!" cried Lucie. "And there's my pinafore!"

Mrs. Tiggy-Winkle ironed the pinafore and shook out the ruffles.

"Oh, that *is* lovely!" said Lucie.

"Are those yellow gloves? asked Lucie.

"Oh, no! That's a pair of stockings belonging to Sally Henny-Penny. Look how she's worn out the heels from scratching in the barnyard! She'll very soon go barefoot!"

"And whose red handkerchief is this?"

"If you please, miss, it belongs to old Mrs. Rabbit. It *did* smell so of onions. I had to wash it separately," said Mrs. Tiggy-Winkle.

"What are these funny white things?" asked Lucie.

"That's a pair of mittens belonging to Tabby Kitten. I only have to iron them, she washes them herself."

"Here are my handkerchiefs!" said Lucie. At last the basket was empty.

After they had sorted the wash, Mrs. Tiggy-Winkle made tea—a cup for herself and a cup for Lucie. She and Lucie sat on a bench in front of the fire and looked at one another.

Mrs. Tiggy-Winkle's hands were very, very brown, and very, very wrinkly from the soapsuds. And all through her gown and cap there were *hairpins* sticking wrong end out.

When they had finished tea, they tied up the clothes in bundles. Lucie's handkerchiefs were folded up inside her clean pinafore and fastened with a silver safety pin.

Then away down the hill trotted Lucie and Mrs. Tiggy-Winkle with the bundles of clothes. All the way down the path little animals came out of the woods to meet them. The very first they met were Peter Rabbit and Benjamin Bunny!

Mrs. Tiggy-Winkle and Lucie gave them all their nice clean clothes. The little animals and birds were very grateful to dear Mrs. Tiggy-Winkle.

At the bottom of the hill they came to the garden steps. There was nothing left to carry except Lucie's one little bundle.

Lucie scrambled up the steps with the bundle in her arms. Then she turned to say "good night" and to thank the washerwoman.

But how *very* odd! Mrs. Tiggy-Winkle had not waited for thanks.

She was running, running, running up the hill—and where was her white ruffled cap? And her shawl? And her gown? And her petticoat?

And how small she seemed—and how brown—and covered with PRICKLES!

Why, Mrs. Tiggy-Winkle was nothing but a HEDGEHOG!

Now some people say that little Lucie had been sleeping and dreaming on the garden steps. But then how could she have found three clean handkerchiefs and a pinafore, all pinned with a silver safety pin?

And besides—I have seen that door in the hill called Cat Bells. And besides—I am a good friend of dear Mrs. Tiggy-Winkle!

THE TALE OF
MR. JEREMY
FISHER

Once upon a time there was a frog named Mr. Jeremy Fisher. He lived in a little damp house among the buttercups at the edge of a pond. The water was all slippy sloppy in his kitchen and by his back door. But Mr. Jeremy liked getting his feet wet. Nobody ever scolded him, and he never caught a cold!

He was quite pleased one day when he looked out and saw large drops of rain splashing in the pond.

"I will get some worms and go fishing and catch a dish of minnows for my dinner," said Jeremy Fisher. "If I catch more than five fish, I will invite Mr. Alderman Ptolemy Tortoise and Sir Isaac Newton to dine with me. Mr. Tortoise, however, eats only salad."

Mr. Jeremy put on a raincoat and a pair of rubber overshoes. He took his fishing rod and basket and set off with enormous hops to the place where he kept his boat.

The boat was round and green and very much like the other lily pads. It was tied to a water plant in the middle of the pond.

Using a twig pole, Mr. Jeremy pushed the lily-pad boat out into open water. "I know a good place for minnows," he said.

Mr. Jeremy stuck his pole into the muddy bottom of the pond and fastened his boat to it. Then he settled himself cross-legged and arranged his fishing tackle. He had the dearest little red bobber. His rod was a tough stalk of grass. His fishing line was a long strand of horsehair. He hooked a little wiggly worm at the end of the line.

The rain trickled down his back, and for nearly an hour he stared at the bobber. "This is getting tiresome," said Mr. Jeremy Fisher. "I think I would like some lunch."

He pushed his boat back among the water grasses at the edge of the pond. Then he took some lunch out of his basket. "I will eat a butterfly sandwich and wait until the shower is over," said Mr. Jeremy Fisher.

Just then a water beetle swam under the lily-pad boat and tweaked Mr. Jeremy's toe! Mr. Jeremy crossed his legs out of reach, and went on eating his butterfly sandwich.

Once or twice something moved about the pond's edge with a rustle and a splash. "I certainly hope that is not a rat," said Mr. Jeremy Fisher. "I think I had better get away from here."

Mr. Jeremy shoved the boat away from shore and dropped in his fishing line. There was a bite almost immediately! The bobber went way under the water! "A minnow! A minnow! I have him by the nose!" cried Mr. Jeremy Fisher, pulling up on his rod.

But what a horrible surprise! Instead of a smooth fat minnow, Mr. Jeremy had caught a huge fish covered with sharp spines! The big fish snapped and flopped about, sticking Mr. Jeremy, until he was quite out of breath.

After the big spiny fish finished flopping around, it jumped back into the water.

A school of minnows put their heads out of the water and laughed at Mr. Jeremy Fisher.

Mr. Jeremy sat sadly on the edge of the lily pad, sucking his sore fingers and peering into the water. Suddenly, a *much* worse thing happened. It would have been a really frightful thing if Mr. Jeremy had not been wearing his raincoat!

An enormous trout jumped—*ker flop-p-p-p!*—with a splash. It seized Mr. Jeremy with a snap!

"Ow! Ow! Ow!" cried Mr. Jeremy. The trout turned and dove to the bottom of the pond!

But the trout didn't like the taste of the raincoat. In less than half a minute it spit Mr. Jeremy out! The only things it swallowed were Mr. Jeremy's rubber overshoes.

Mr. Jeremy bobbed up to the surface of the water like a cork. He swam with all his might to the edge of the pond. He scrambled out of the water and hopped home across the meadow with his raincoat in tatters.

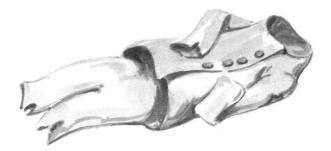

"What a mercy that was not an even bigger fish!" said Mr. Jeremy. "I have lost my rod and basket, but it does not much matter. I am sure I will never dare to go fishing again!"

That evening he bandaged his fingers and invited his friends to dinner. He could not offer them fish, but he had something else in the pantry.

His guests soon arrived. Sir Isaac Newton wore his black and gold waistcoat. Mr. Alderman Ptolemy Tortoise brought a salad with him in a string bag.

Instead of a nice dish of minnows, Mr. Jeremy served Mr. Tortoise and Sir Isaac Newton a roasted grasshopper with ladybug sauce for dinner. Frogs consider it a beautiful treat, but I think it would have been awful!

THE TALE OF

PIGLING

BLAND

Once upon a time there was an old pig named Aunt Pettitoes. She had four little girl pigs, named Cross-Patch, Wee-One, Yock-Yock, and Spot. And she had four little boy pigs, named Alexander, Pigling Bland, Chin-Chin, and Stumpy.

One day, Aunt Pettitoes said, "It is time for all of you to make your way in the world." So all her piglets, except Pigling Bland, rode away in a cart.

"Now, Pigling Bland, take these work papers to market so someone will hire you. Stay away from traps, hen roosts, and bacon and eggs. Remember to always walk upon your back legs." Aunt Pettitoes gave him a little lunch and eight peppermint candies. Then she waved him on his way.

Pigling Bland trotted down the road. To pass the time, he sang,

"This little pig went to market,
This little pig stayed home,
This little pig had roast beef. . ."

The song made Pigling Bland hungry. So he sat down and ate his lunch—every bit. He ate two of his eight peppermints, too. After his rest, Pigling Bland walked a little farther. He came to a sign that read: To Market, 5 miles; Over the Hills, 4 miles.

Pigling Bland thought he would never get to market before dark. He decided to take the shorter way over the hills. He walked and walked. It began to grow dark outside. The wind whistled and the trees creaked and groaned. He took several wrong turns, and was soon quite lost. He was frightened and cried, "Wee, wee, wee! I can't find my way home!"

Finally, Pigling Bland saw a hen house. He hurried inside. "What else can I do?" asked Pigling.

"Bacon and eggs!" clucked a hen.

"Trap, trap, trap!" warned a rooster.

"To market, to market, jiggetty jig!" clucked another hen, a red one.

Just then, a man came to catch six chickens to take to market. His name was Mr. Piperson. He caught a white hen. Then he saw Pigling Bland squeezed up in a corner.

"What is this?" he exclaimed. "A pig! Just right for bacon and eggs!" He grabbed Pigling Bland and dropped him into a cage. Then he dropped in five more smelly, cackling hens.

Pigling Bland was nearly scratched to pieces.

At last Pigling Bland was lifted out of the cage. "What a find!" said Mr. Piperson. "You can sleep on the rug in front of the fire."

In the morning, Mr. Piperson made oatmeal. He poured it into three bowls. One was for himself, one was for Pigling Bland, and one was for. . .?

Mr. Piperson glared at Pigling, so Pigling looked away. Mr. Piperson opened a closet door and walked in. He came out without the third bowl of oatmeal. He gobbled down his own breakfast and left for market with the six hens.

Pigling went on tiptoe to the locked door. He sniffed at the keyhole. All was quiet. Pigling pushed a peppermint under the door. It disappeared immediately! Pigling pushed the rest of his peppermints under the door.

When Mr. Piperson returned that night, he made more oatmeal. Again he took a bowl into the closet. But he didn't shut the door carefully. When he locked it, it didn't really lock. Then Mr. Piperson went to bed.

Pigling Bland sat by the fire and ate his supper. All at once, a little voice said, "My name is Pig-Wig. Make me more oatmeal, please!"

Pigling Bland nearly jumped out of his skin! A lovely little black pig stood smiling beside him. She pointed to Pigling's bowl. He quickly gave it to her. "How did you get here?" he asked.

"I was stolen for bacon and hams," replied Pig-Wig, with her mouth full.

"Stolen!" exclaimed Pigling Bland. "Oh, how terrible. Why don't you run away?"

"I will after supper," replied Pig-Wig. After she finished her second bowl of oatmeal, Pig-Wig got up to leave.

"You can't go in the dark," said Pigling Bland, "but if you wait until morning, I shall help you run away."

They agreed to wait until they could see the first light of day. With that taken care of, Pig-Wig settled in for a good night's sleep. Poor Pigling Bland was nervous. He stayed awake the whole night sitting in front of the fire. He sat there listening to make sure he could hear the snores Mr. Piperson made while sleeping.

They left early the next morning. The sun rose, and from the top of a hill they saw a bridge. They knew they'd be safe once they crossed it. Pigling heard a noise. A grocer was coming along in his wagon.

"Leave the talking to me," whispered Pigling. "We may have to make a run for it." He pretended to be hurt and held Pig-Wig's arm.

"Two little pigs! Just right for bacon!" said the grocer. "Do you have working papers?" Pigling handed up his papers.

"These take care of you," said the grocer, "but they do not say anything about the girl pig." He saw a farmer plowing a nearby field. "Maybe she belongs to that farmer," the grocer said. "Wait here while I go ask him." The grocer drove off. A hurt pig could not run away.

"Now, Pig-Wig! Run NOW!" cried Pigling Bland.

Never did two pigs run as fast as these pigs ran! They raced and squealed and pelted down the hill toward the bridge. Pig-Wig's petticoats fluttered, and her feet went *pitter, patter, pitter.* They ran, ran, ran down the hill!

They came to the river,
They came to the bridge,
They crossed it hand in hand—
Then over the hills and far away . . .
Pig-Wig danced with Pigling Bland!

THE TALE OF

GINGER & PICKLES

Once there was a little shop called "Ginger & Pickles." The shop was just the right size for dolls. Lucinda and Jane, who lived in the dollhouse, always bought their groceries at Ginger and Pickles. The counter inside was also just the right height for rabbits.

Ginger and Pickles sold red spotted handkerchiefs, sugar, and galoshes. The shop sold nearly everything, except for a few things you might want in a hurry— like shoelaces, hairpins, and lamb chops.

Ginger and Pickles were the owners of the shop. Ginger was a yellow tomcat and Pickles was a dog.

The rabbits who came into the shop were always a little bit afraid of Pickles. The mice were rather fearful of Ginger. Ginger usually asked Pickles to help the mice, because he said helping the mice made him hungry.

"I cannot bear to see them going out the door carrying their little packages," said Ginger.

"I have the same feeling about rabbits," replied Pickles. "But it would not be right to eat our own customers. They would leave us and go to Tabitha Twitchit's store."

"Actually, they wouldn't shop anywhere any more if that happened," replied Ginger gloomily.

Tabitha Twitchit ran the only other shop in the village. And she did not give credit.

Ginger and Pickles gave unlimited credit.

Now the meaning of "credit" is this: If a customer buys a bar of soap, instead of paying for it right away, she says she will pay another time. Pickles, being a very kind sort, makes a low bow and says, "With pleasure, madam." Then Pickles carefully writes the amount of owed money in a book. The records for all the items bought on credit were kept in this book.

Customers came again and again, and bought a lot, in spite of being afraid of Ginger and Pickles. Everyone liked to use the credit that Ginger and Pickles let them have. But there was no money in the money drawer. Day in and day out, lots and lots of customers came and went. But they never paid as much as a penny for peppermints!

And as there was never any money, Ginger and Pickles had to eat food from the shop. Pickles ate biscuits and Ginger ate canned fish. They would eat their dinner by candlelight after the shop was closed for the day.

The first of January came around. As Ginger and Pickles looked over their record-keeping books, they realized they still had no money. Poor Pickles was unable to buy a dog license. He was not able to walk around outside without a dog license.

"It is very unpleasant," Pickles told Ginger. "I am afraid of the police."

"It is your own fault for being a dog. Being a cat, *I* do not need a license," replied Ginger.

"I am afraid I will be arrested. I have tried to buy a license on credit at City Hall, but they do not give credit there," said Pickles. "The place is full of police officers, too. I met one as I was coming home."

"Let's send another bill to Samuel Whiskers. He owes us quite a lot for bacon," sighed Ginger.

"Let's send *everyone* their bills again," said Pickles.

Ginger and Pickles went into their room in back of the store. There they worked on the bills. It was quiet as they added up numbers, numbers, numbers.

After a while they heard a noise in the front of the shop. As Ginger and Pickles walked to the front of the store, they were surprised at what they saw. An envelope was on the counter, and a police officer doll was writing in a notebook! Pickles nearly had a fit. He barked and barked!

"Bite him, Pickles!" called Ginger from behind a sugar barrel. "He's only a doll!"

The police officer doll kept writing in his notebook. Pickles kept on barking and barking until he finally just gave up.

When it was all quiet, Pickles found the shop was empty. The officer had disappeared. But the envelope was still on the counter. Ginger walked over to the counter and picked up the envelope. Pickles was becoming very worried about the whole situation.

"Do you think he has gone to get a real live police officer?" Pickles asked Ginger. "I am afraid the letter says I must go to court."

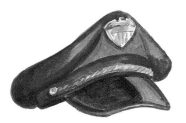

"No, you do not need to go to court," answered Ginger, who had opened the envelope. After carefully reading the rest of the letter, Ginger announced, "It is a tax bill."

Pickles was upset. They had no money for the things they already needed. Now they were going to have to pay taxes, too. "This is the last straw," said Pickles. "Let's close the shop." So Ginger and Pickles locked the door and shutters, and left. The closing of the shop caused many problems.

Tabitha Twitchit immediately raised the price of everything in her store by a penny. And still she refused to give credit.

Everyone was pleased when Sally Henny-Penny put up posters to say that she was going to reopen Ginger and Pickle's shop. The posters said, "Henny's Grand Opening Sale! Penny's penny prices! Come try, come buy!" The posters made everyone want to visit the new shop.

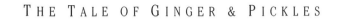

On opening day the shop was filled with customers.

Sally Henny-Penny gets rather nervous when she tries to count out change, and she does insist on being paid in cash. But she is quite harmless.

And her store has a remarkable assortment of bargains. There is something to please everybody!

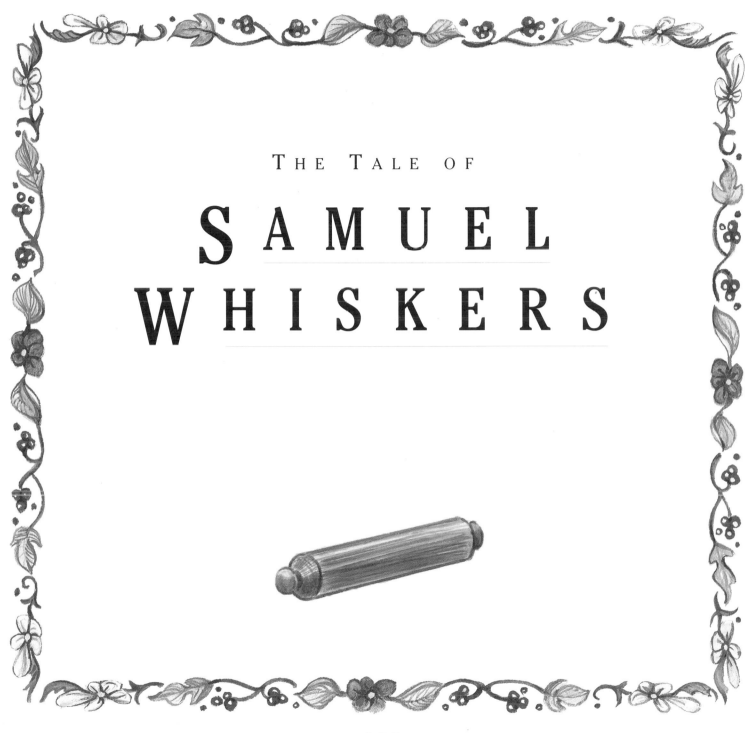

THE TALE OF

SAMUEL WHISKERS

Once upon a time, Mrs. Tabitha Twitchit, the anxious mother of three kittens, decided to keep them out of mischief on baking day. She caught Moppet and Mittens and shut them up in a cupboard, but little Tom could not be found.

Mrs. Tabitha searched upstairs and down, mewing for her lost son. It was an old, creaky house, full of hiding places, passages, and odd little doorways—and maybe even a secret staircase behind the wall. Things were always disappearing at night, like cheese and bacon.

Moppet and Mittens managed to escape from the cupboard. At that moment there came a knock at the front door.

It was the neighbor, Mrs. Ribby, who had come to borrow some yeast. Tabitha greeted her tearfully.

"I've lost dear Thomas," she mewed. "I'm afraid the rats have gotten him!" She told how she had looked everywhere for her kitten. "What a thing it is to have an unruly family!"

Mrs. Ribby offered to help look. The two found Moppet and Mittens gone, too. Now they began searching all over again, poking under beds with Ribby's umbrella, rummaging through cupboards, and searching the clothes chest in the attic. Tabitha complained about the rat problem.

Back in the kitchen, they found Moppet hiding in the flour barrel.

"Mother," cried Moppet, "I saw an old woman rat stealing some dough!" Next, they found Mittens at the bottom of a big jar. She, too, had seen something—an old man rat carrying off a pat of butter and a rolling pin.

"Didn't we hear a roly-poly noise in the attic?" Ribby wondered. She and Tabitha rushed upstairs, where they could hear the noise quite clearly under the floorboards.

"This is serious," Ribby declared. "You must send for John Joiner, the carpenter!"

But whatever had become of Tom Kitten?

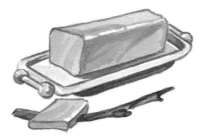

Tom did not want to be shut away in a cupboard, so he had hidden in the chimney above the stove. It was big enough for a man, so there was plenty of room for a little tomcat.

Still, the air was smoky and the fire below was scary. Afraid of scorching his lovely little tail, Tom decided to climb out the chimney, right onto the roof tiles. There, he might catch a sparrow or two. The chimney was made of stone and topped by slanting slates that kept out the rain but also let in daylight.

Tom climbed up, and up, and up some more. Then he waded sideways through inches of soot until he was quite filthy.

Tom kept climbing until he found a loosened stone in the wall and meat bones lying around.

"How funny!" cried Tom. "Who would be gnawing on bones up here? And that smell—it's like a mouse, only awfully strong!"

He squeezed through a hole in the wall and went down a tight passageway. By now, Tom was in the attic, although he didn't know it. All at once, he fell down a hole and landed on a heap of dirty rags in a small, stuffy room—across from an enormous rat.

"What do you mean by tumbling into my bed?" squeaked the rat. "Anna Maria! Anna Maria!"

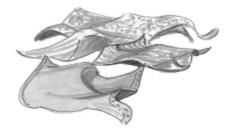

An old woman rat came into the room. In a twinkling, she pounced on little Tom, pulled off his jacket, rolled him up, and tied him with string.

"Anna Maria," said Samuel Whiskers (for that was the old man rat's name), "make this creature into a roly-poly pudding for dinner!"

"I'll need dough, butter, and a rolling pin," said his wife.

And that was the reason Samuel Whiskers came downstairs to get the pat of butter and rolling pin, and why Anna Maria stole the bit of bread dough.

Left alone, Tom wriggled and squirmed and tried to mew, but his mouth was full of soot and cobwebs. A spider came to look, but offered no help. Soon the two rats returned to smear Tom with butter and roll him in dough.

"How can we avoid eating the string?" asked Samuel Whiskers. But his wife was too busy holding Tom still. The rolling pin went roly-poly, roly-poly, until all that showed of the kitten was the head and tail.

Suddenly, there came the sounds of sawing overhead, and a dog scratching and yelping. The rats dropped the rolling pin and scurried away.

And so Tom was rescued just in time by the carpenter. John Joiner spent the rest of the morning sniffing around the hole he'd made in the floor. The roly-poly dough was saved and baked into a currant pudding, and the kitten was given a hot bath to get the butter off.

Meanwhile, Samuel Whiskers and his wife ran away from the Twitchit house with all their belongings in a wheelbarrow they had stolen. The pair turned in at the gate to Farmer Potatoes' land. Once inside his barn, they began hauling their luggage and packages to the top of a mound of hay.

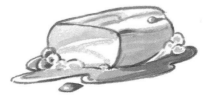

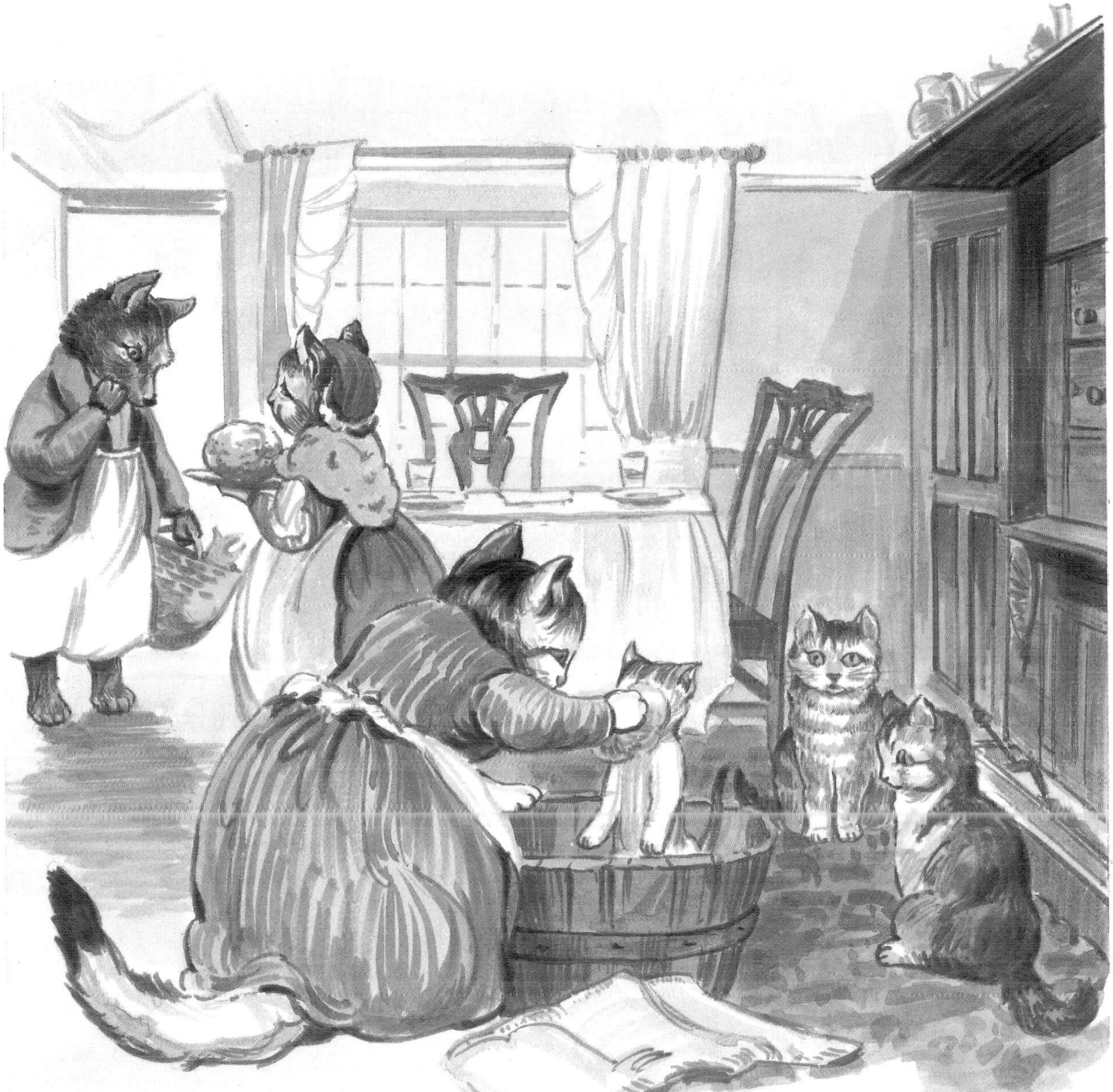

For a long time after that, the rats stayed away from the Twitchits' house. But there was no happy ending for Farmer Potatoes. Everywhere he looked, there were rats and more rats! It nearly drove him crazy that he could not get rid of them. (As you've probably guessed, they were all the children, grandchildren, and great-grandchildren of Samuel and Anna Maria Whiskers.)

In time, Moppet and Mittens grew up to be excellent rat catchers. They hired themselves out, charging by the dozen. There was always plenty of work, so they earned a good living. To advertise their skill, they would hang rats' tails on the barn door.

As for Tom Kitten, his was a different story. Far from chasing rats, he was deathly afraid of them for the rest of his life. In fact, he never dared to face anything larger than a mouse!

THE TALE OF
MRS.
TITTLEMOUSE

Once upon a time there was a wood-mouse called Mrs. Tittlemouse.

Her house was built in a bank under a hedge, and such a funny house it was! There were yards and yards of sandy passages that led to storerooms and nut cellars and seed cellars, all among the roots of the hedge.

The house had a kitchen, a front room for guests, and two pantries. There was also, of course, Mrs. Tittlemouse's bedroom, where she slept in a little box bed.

Mrs. Tittlemouse was an extremely tidy person. She was always sweeping and dusting the floors. Once in a while, a beetle would lose its way in the long, winding passages.

"Shoo! Shoo! with your dirty little feet!" Mrs. Tittlemouse would cry, clattering her dust pan and brush at the creature.

One day, quite by accident, a ladybug paid Mrs. Tittlemouse a visit. She was quickly chased away.

"Fly away home to your children!" cried Mrs. Tittlemouse.

Mrs. Tittlemouse went to a faraway storeroom to get some cherry pits and thistledown seed for dinner. Along the passage she sniffed the odor of honey.

"Hmmmmm! I'm sure I see the marks of dirty little feet!"

Around the corner sat Babbitty Bumble.

"Zizz, bizz, bizz!" said the bumble bee in greeting.

"Good day, Babbitty Bumble," replied Mrs. Tittlemouse. "Why are you down here? Why do you always come in through a window and then say, 'Zizz, bizz, bizz'?" Mrs. Tittlemouse was getting cross.

Babbitty Bumble disappeared into a room that at one time had stored acorns. The room should have been empty, but it was full of untidy dried moss.

When Mrs. Tittlemouse began pulling out the moss, three or four bees stuck their heads out, buzzing fiercely.

"I'm not in the habit of renting rooms!" said Mrs. Tittlemouse sharply. "However shall I get rid of them? Who will help?"

She thought about asking Mr. Jackson, but the toad lived in a drain below the hedge and never wiped his feet. She left the bees and returned upstairs—only to find Mr. Jackson sitting in her rocking chair!

"How do you do, Mr. Jackson? My, but you're wet!" said Mrs. Tittlemouse.

"I'm quite well, thank you, thank you," said the toad. "May I sit awhile and dry out?" And so he sat and smiled as water dripped off the hem of his coat.

The polite Mrs. Tittlemouse offered him some dinner. But the toad had no teeth (as proof, he opened his mouth unnecessarily wide).

"Thank you, thank you, but what I'd really like is a dish of honey!" he said.

"I have none in the house," Mrs. Tittlemouse said.

"Tiddly, widdly, widdly," said Mr. Jackson. "Why, I can smell it! That is why I came to visit!"

The toad rose heavily from the table and began searching the cupboards. Mrs. Tittlemouse was close behind with a rag, wiping up his wet foot marks. When Mr. Jackson found no honey there, he waddled down the passage.

"You'll get stuck," warned Mrs. Tittlemouse.

But the toad just spoke a few tiddly-widdlies and kept searching.

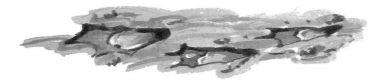

A butterfly, perched on a lump of sugar, flew away.

"You have a lot of visitors, Mrs. Tittlemouse!" remarked the toad.

"And with no invitation!" said the mouse.

Down the sandy passage, the two met up with Babbitty Bumble. Now, Mr. Jackson did not like bumble bees. But then, bees were not awfully fond of *him*.

"Get out, you nasty old toad!" shrieked Babbitty Bumble.

"I will go crazy!" wept Mrs. Tittlemouse. She hid in the nut cellar while Mr. Jackson pulled out the bees' nest. When she came out, everyone had gone and left a dreadful mess. Moss, thistledown, smears of honey, dirty footprints—oh, it was horrible!

Mrs. Tittlemouse gathered up the moss and what was left of the beeswax. Then she went out and fetched some twigs to partly close up the front door and make it too tight a squeeze for Mr. Jackson. She got some soap, rags, and a scrub brush, but was too tired to go on. So she took a nap in her chair.

"Will my house ever be tidy again?" the poor mouse fretted.

She went to bed. Next day, she got up early and began a spring cleaning that took two weeks. She swept and scrubbed and dusted and waxed and polished—

—Until finally everything was beautifully neat and clean and shining. To celebrate, Mrs. Tittlemouse gave a party for five other little mice. Mr. Jackson was not sent an invitation.

Even so, the toad smelled the party from his home in the drain below the hedge. He came up the bank, but because of the twigs, he could not squeeze through the doorway.

The mice decided to be nice to the toad, however.

Through the window, they handed him acorn cups of honeydew, and he was not at all bothered.

Mr. Jackson sat outside in the sun and raised a toast: "Tiddly, widdly, widdly! To your good health, Mrs. Tittlemouse!"

THE TALE OF THE
PIE & THE
PATTY-PAN

Once upon a time, Ribby the cat invited a little dog named Duchess to tea.

"Come soon," wrote Ribby, "and we will have something delicious, which I am baking in a pie dish with a pink rim. You shall have it all, my dear friend, and I will eat only muffins."

Duchess wrote back: "I will be there promptly at a quarter past four." She almost added: "I hope it won't be mouse," but realized this would be too rude. Duchess had a veal-and-ham pie in a pink-edged dish just like Ribby's. The little dog liked it much better than mouse meat.

Then Duchess had an idea. Ribby would surely go out to buy her muffins. Why not use that time to replace her friend's mouse-meat pie with the veal-and-ham one? After all, the two dishes looked just alike. How clever of Duchess!

Meanwhile, Ribby was popping *her* pie into the oven—the bottom oven, since the top one would bake too quickly. It was indeed a mouse pie, most delicate and tender, with all the bones removed.

"I don't want Duchess to choke. She does eat fast," said Ribby to herself, "though she *is* quite a nice and elegant little dog!"

Ribby then got busy dusting and polishing, shaking the rabbit-skin rug, and setting the table. She fetched milk and butter from the farm. Finally, she set out for the village to buy tea, sugar, and marmalade.

At that moment, Duchess was on her way to Ribby's with the veal-and-ham pie hidden in a basket. The two friends crossed paths and only nodded, since they would see each other later.

Her shopping finished, Ribby went home. Entering the front door, she heard a noise at the back of the house.

"Thank goodness I locked up the silver spoons!" she exclaimed. But no burglar could be found.

The noise, of course, was Duchess, leaving by the back door.

"It's a very odd thing that Ribby's pie was *not* in the oven when I put mine in," she growled to herself as she trotted home. "I cannot think where she put it!"

Meanwhile, Ribby prepared for the party by changing into her lilac silk gown and making the tea. She peeked at her pie, which was browning nicely.

At four on the dot and carrying a bunch of flowers between her teeth, Duchess set out for her friend's.

"I wonder if Ribby has taken my pie out of the oven yet!" she fretted.

At four-fifteen came a little tap-tap at Ribby's door.

"Is Mrs. Ribston at home?" barked Duchess politely.

"Come in, my dear Duchess, and how do you do?" Ribby replied. She poured tea for her friend. The little dog asked for a lump of sugar, and then balanced it on her nose.

"How sweetly you beg!" said Ribby.

But the sugar lump dropped to the floor, and Duchess ducked under the table to look for it. And so, she did not see Ribby take the pie from the *bottom* oven. The two sat down, and Ribby began slicing the pie.

"Look out for the patty-pan!" warned Duchess. She had carefully put a patty-pan in her pie.

"Beg pardon?" Ribby asked. She owned four of these little tin dishes, which cooks often put in the middle of a pie to hold up the crust. Duchess had wolfed down four helpings of pie and was now scraping around in the dish.

"I was only feeling for the patty-pan," the little dog explained.

"There is none," said Ribby. "It is not needed in mouse pies."

"I shall die! I shall die! I have swallowed a patty-pan!" wailed Duchess. "Oh, I do feel ill!"

"Nonsense," said Ribby. Still, she was a bit worried.

"Shall I fetch Dr. Maggotty?" Ribby suggested. "Let me first lock up the spoons."

She settled Duchess in an armchair by the fire and hurried to the village. She found the magpie doctor at the blacksmith's, dropping rusty nails into an ink bottle.

"Gammon? ha! HA!" he screeched, in the language of his kind.

Ribby explained that Duchess had swallowed a patty-pan and was ill.

"Spinach? ha! HA!" he answered.

The cat and the bird rushed back through the village, making a spectacle for all to see.

While Ribby was away, Duchess checked the pie again for a patty-pan. Then she heard something siz-z-z-le! She opened the *top* oven and smelled the rich aroma of veal and ham baking. Through a hole in the crust, she glimpsed a tin patty-pan.

"Why, I must have been eating mouse meat!" she cried. "No wonder I feel ill! Of course, I would feel much worse if I had really swallowed a patty-pan!"

Duchess set her pie outside the back door so she could sneak it home later.

Ribby and Dr. Maggotty arrived to find Duchess feeling much better. The magpie held a pill in his beak, which the dog took with a glass of milk.

Since his patient was feeling better, Dr. Maggotty left. Duchess said she, too, should go. But once Ribby's door shut, the little dog scampered around back—only to find Dr. Maggotty and three grackles eating her pie. Feeling very silly, she ran all the way home.

Later, when Ribby came out to pump water, she found a pink-edged pie dish smashed to bits. Nearby was a little patty-pan.

"So, there really *was* a patty-pan," she thought. "But mine are all in the kitchen cupboard, and. . ." At last, she understood what had happened. "Why, of all the nerve!"

It would be a long while before Duchess was invited to tea at Ribby's again!

THE
TAILOR OF
GLOUCESTER

A long time ago, there lived an old tailor in Gloucester town. He worked from morning till dark, sewing and snipping for others. He himself was poor and wore threadbare clothes.

One cold day before Christmas, the tailor began a cherry-colored silk coat embroidered with pansies and roses for the Mayor.

When the snow began falling against the windowpanes, the tailor put down his work, for the day was done. Everything was in order and measured exactly. The only thing left to do was to buy some cherry-colored silk thread for the final buttonhole of the vest.

The tailor went home after first closing the window, locking the shop door, and taking the key. No one lived there at night but little brown mice, and they came and went freely through little trap doors and underground passageways that connected the houses in Gloucester.

The tailor came home to the room that he shared with his cat, Simpkin.

"Meow," said the cat when his master entered. The tailor was tired from his work. He sent Simpkin to buy a few things for supper—and a bit of cherry-colored silk thread to finish the Mayor's vest the next day.

After the cat left, the tailor sat down near the fireplace, talking to himself about the embroidered coat and vest. Suddenly, he jumped up. Little noises—*tip tap, tip tap, tip tap tip!*—came from the hutch where he kept his dishes.

The tailor went to look. Again, from under a teacup, came the little noises. He lifted it up, and out stepped a little lady mouse. She curtsied and scampered away.

The tailor sat down again and talked to himself about the Mayor's coat and vest. Once again he heard little noises—*tip tap, tip tap, tip tap tip!*—from the hutch.

"This is extraordinary!" he exclaimed.

The tailor turned over another teacup, and out stepped a little gentleman mouse. He bowed and scampered away. Then came a chorus of little tappings. Out from under teacups and bowls came many little mice, who hopped down and scurried away.

The tailor returned to his chair and began muttering about the work to be done on the coat and vest. All the mice came out again to listen and whisper. Then they ran away, down the passages between the houses, until not one was left in the tailor's kitchen.

When Simpkin returned, the tailor asked, "Where is my thread? Where is my thread?"

Simpkin set down his packages, but secretly hid one in the teapot. He growled and spit at the tailor, and if he had been able to talk, he would have said, "Where is my *mouse*?" For he had been expecting dinner.

"Oh, I am ruined without the thread!" cried the tailor, and he sadly went to bed.

All night, Simpkin searched for mice, but could find none. By morning, the tailor was ill with a fever and could not work. In fact, he stayed in bed for three days and nights. What would become of the Mayor's coat and vest?

At midnight on Chistmas Eve, the clock struck, and Simpkin set out to wander the snowy streets.

Under the eaves of houses sang starlings and sparrows. Grackles awoke in the cathedral tower, and robins began to chirp all over town. All this made poor Simpkin very hungry indeed!

Most surprising was a glow of light that seemed to be coming from the tailor's shop. When Simpkin crept up to peep in at the window, he found the shop filled with lighted candles.

The air was filled with the sound of scissors snipping and thread snapping and little mouse voices singing.

"Mew, mew!" said Simpkin, and he scratched at the door. The key was back at home, under the tailor's pillow, so he could not get in.

The little mice only laughed and sang a new song.

"Mew, mew!" said Simpkin again. But the mice ignored him. They simply clicked away with their needles and thimbles. When the cat scratched at the windowsill, the mice closed the shutters on him and went back to their sewing!

When Simpkin went home, he found the tailor feeling much better and sleeping peacefully. The cat went on tip-toe to the teapot and took out the package he had hidden. It was the cherry-colored silk thread the tailor needed so badly. Simpkin felt ashamed for having hidden it.

When the tailor awoke on Christmas morning, the first thing he saw on the quilt was a bit of cherry-colored thread. Beside the bed stood his apologetic cat.

Happily, the tailor got dressed and went to his shop, with Simpkin running before him. He thought he would work on the coat and vest, though he could not hope to finish them on time.

But there on the table—oh joy!—was the loveliest cherry-colored silk coat ever worn by a mayor of Gloucester, and a satin vest embroidered all over with flowers. Everything was perfect except for one little detail: the last buttonhole on the vest. Pinned to the cloth was a note with the teeniest script:

NO MORE THREAD

Gratefully, the tailor finished the buttonhole.

From that day forward, his luck improved, and he grew quite rich. He made the most wonderful coats for the wealthy citizens of Gloucester—and for fine gentlemen all over England!

What made his handiwork so special was the buttonholes. The stitches were so small you could not help but wonder how an old man with crooked fingers could have made them. The stitches were *so* small that they might have been made by little mice!

THE TALE OF

MR. TOD

This is the story of two *very* disagreeable persons, Mr. Tod and Tommy Brock.

Mr. Tod was a red fox who was no friend of the rabbits. He owned half a dozen houses and changed them often. When he moved out of one house, Tommy Brock the badger might move in, without permission.

Tommy was short, fat, and dirty. He ate wasp nests and frogs and worms—and, once in a while, rabbit pie. One day, he paid old Mr. Bouncer a friendly visit while the rabbit's son Benjamin Bunny and daughter-in-law Flopsy were away. Mr. Bouncer was supposed to watch their babies, but he often forgot things.

Tommy Brock complained that he hadn't had a good meal in weeks. "I suppose I shall have to eat my own tail!" he joked. Mr. Bouncer treated his hungry friend to seed cake and cowslip wine. Afterward, they smoked cabbage-leaf cigars.

The old rabbit fell asleep in his chair, and when Benjamin and Flopsy returned, their babies were gone! Though Mr. Bouncer would not admit he'd had a guest, the smell of badger was quite strong. Benjamin Bunny set off after Tommy Brock.

Late in the day, Benjamin came upon a rabbit in a blue coat. "Cousin Peter Rabbit!" he cried.

Benjamin told Peter Rabbit how Tommy Brock had taken his young family. "Seven babies, Cousin Peter, and all of them twins!"

"Yes, I just saw Tommy carrying a sack with something alive in it," Peter said. He offered to help Benjamin find his children before they became the badger's breakfast. "What a nasty person!"

After much walking, they came upon one of Mr. Tod's many homes—this one at the top of Bull Banks. The house, a cross between a prison and a pigsty, was shut up tight. Through the window, though, they glimpsed the kitchen. The fireplace was neatly laid with sticks, ready for lighting.

At one end of the table were an empty pie dish, a carving knife, and a chopper. There was also a place setting. Benjamin gave a shudder. At the next window, they saw someone asleep in Mr. Tod's bed. But where were the babies?

After sunset, the cousins saw many unpleasant things lying around on the ground—rabbit bones and skulls and chicken legs. It was most shocking!

Later, by moonlight, they could make out the iron door of a little wall oven in the kitchen. And then they knew: The babies were shut up live in the oven, ready to be cooked at breakfast!

What to do? After much whispering, they decided to dig a tunnel under the house. By sunrise, they had scratched their way under the kitchen. Then all of a sudden, they heard the bark of a fox. The cousins trembled in the dark tunnel.

Mr. Tod was in a terrible mood. He had failed to catch a pheasant in her nest, and two of her eggs had been bad. As usual, when he felt low, he would change houses, so he was returning to Bull Banks. On the way, he noticed badger tracks. In the kitchen, he was furious to see the table set for a meal.

Mr. Tod heard snoring from the bedroom. His whiskers bristled with rage. Tommy Brock was flat on his back in bed—*and* with his boots on!

Mr. Tod thought about what punishment would be best. He went to get a clothesline with a hook at one end. The fox put the other end out the bedroom window, then tied the rope to a tree in the yard. (Tommy had been watching all along, but was too lazy to move. So he pretended to sleep.)

Mr. Tod returned with a pail of water. This he put down while he arranged the hooked end of the line over the bed's canopy.

Mr. Tod had planned to hang the pail of water above his unwelcome guest's head, then spill it by pulling on the rope from the yard. But the pail was too heavy to lift. So he emptied it and hung it from the hook. Then he ladled in water from a jug. A drop or two splashed on Tommy, but the badger never budged.

"It will make a great mess," thought Mr. Tod, "but the bedding needs cleaning anyway."

When Mr. Tod left, Tommy rolled the fox's robe into a bundle and stuck it beneath the sheet. Then he lit the kitchen fire and made tea.

In the yard, Mr. Tod gnawed through the rope, and from the house came a crash and the sound of a pail rolling over and over. But no screams. From the window, the fox could see the soggy bed. The lumpy shape beneath the sheet never moved.

"I've killed him dead!" said Mr. Tod happily. "I'll bury him and then do a good spring cleaning!"

But this was not to be. Tommy Brock, very much alive, sat grinning and drinking tea at the kitchen table. He threw a cup of hot tea at Mr. Tod when the fox came through the door.

Benjamin and Peter crept out from the tunnel when they heard the sounds of fighting overhead. It was a most fearful fight—plates smashing, pots and pans crashing, furniture breaking, windows shattering.

The fox and the badger then rolled out the door together and kept on fighting, snarling, and thrashing. They fell over the bank, down the hill, and into the rocks. Oh, those two will never be friends!

Benjamin ran back and rescued his babies. He and Peter hurried home, half carrying, half dragging the sack of warm, wiggly bunnies. They did not stop to listen to the sounds of fighting that still echoed in the woods.

We, too, can only guess how the terrible battle between Mr. Tod and Tommy Brock ended.

THE TALE OF
JOHNNY
TOWN-MOUSE

Johnny Town-Mouse was born in a cupboard. Timmy Willie—who was a country-mouse—was born in a garden.

One day, Timmy Willie was sent to town by mistake in a vegetable basket. You see, he had crept into it and fallen fast asleep after eating some peas. Every week the basket was loaded into a cart and taken to town.

Timmy Willie awoke with a fright. The basket was jolted this way and that, and the little country-mouse trembled among the jumbled-up vegetables.

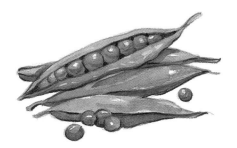

At last, the cart stopped at a house. The basket was taken out, carried in, and set down. But there was no peace for Timmy Willie. Dogs barked, boys whistled in the street, the maid hurried upstairs and down, and the canary sang like a steam engine. As soon as the cook opened the basket, out sprang the little country-mouse.

"A mouse! A mouse!" cried the cook. She jumped up on a chair. "Get the cat! And hand me a poker from the fireplace!"

Timmy Willie rushed along the edge of the room. He found a hole in the wall and ducked inside.

He dropped right into the middle of a mouse dinner table and broke three glasses.

"Who in the world is this?" asked Johnny Town-Mouse, forgetting his manners for a moment. Recovering them quickly, he made introductions. All the mice at the party had long tails and white neckties. Timmy Willie's tail was nothing much to speak of. The others noticed, but were too polite to mention it.

The dinner was simple yet elegant, with eight courses. Timmy Willie, who was asked to join, was so nervous he dropped a plate.

"Never mind," said Johnny Town-Mouse kindly.

"Where are the youngsters with dessert?" he then asked. It was the job of two younger mice to find food in the kitchen upstairs, grab it, run from the cat, and serve it to the party-goers. Once he learned about the cat, Timmy Willie nearly fainted.

"Try some jelly?" offered Johnny Town-Mouse. "No? Would you rather go to bed?"

He showed Timmy Willie a sofa pillow with a hole in it. But the sofa smelled of cat, so Timmy Willie slept under the fireplace fender.

Timmy Willie was dreadfully homesick. He missed his peaceful nest on the sunny bank. He hated town food. Noises kept him awake at night. One day, he described his country home to Johnny Town-Mouse.

"It sounds rather dull," his host remarked.

Timmy Willie explained how he would sit in his sandy burrow and shell corn and seeds and tend his garden of roses, pinks, and pansies.

"There goes that cat again!" Johnny Town-Mouse cried, when a noise interrupted them. "I'm sorry you haven't enjoyed our hospitality."

"Oh, you have been most kind," said Timmy Willie, "but I do feel so ill."

"Perhaps, then, you should return in the basket," Johnny Town-Mouse suggested.

"Oh? Oh!" cried Timmy Willie.

"Didn't you know the basket goes back empty every Saturday?" asked the town-mouse.

And so, Timmy Willie said goodbye to his friends and hid in the basket with a bit of cake and cabbage to eat during the trip.

Sometimes, on Saturdays, Timmy Willie would look for Johnny Town-Mouse, who had half-promised to visit. But no one ever jumped out of the hamper.

Winter passed, and spring came again. Timmy Willie sat by his burrow, smelling the violets and new grass—when up the sandy path all spick-and-span with a brown leather bag came Johnny Town-Mouse!

Timmy Willie was overjoyed. He invited his friend to sit in the sun and eat herb pudding.

"Hmmm, it is a bit damp," said Johnny Town-Mouse, holding his tail above the mud. "What is that fearful noise?"

"That? Why, it's just a harmless cow," replied Timmy Willie. "How are all our friends?"

Johnny Town-Mouse's story was not very interesting. He was paying the country-mouse a visit at this time only because the family had gone to the seaside for Easter, and the cook was doing spring cleaning—with instructions to clear out all the mice. There were four kittens, and the cat had killed the canary.

"They say we did it, but I know better," said Johnny Town-Mouse. "What's that dreadful racket?"

"Just the lawn mower," replied Timmy Willie. "I'll fetch some grass clippings for your bed. You ought to settle in the country, Johnny."

"We'll see about that, Timmy Willie," said his guest. "The basket will be going back in a few days, as soon as the family returns from the seaside."

"I am certain that you will never want to live in town again, once you have tasted the delights of country living," Timmy Willie replied.

But that turned out not to be the case. Johnny Town-Mouse went back in the very next basket of vegetables. He said the countryside was too quiet!

One place suits one person, another place suits another person—although many of us might prefer to live in the country, like Timmy Willie!

THE TALE OF

TIMMY
TIPTOES

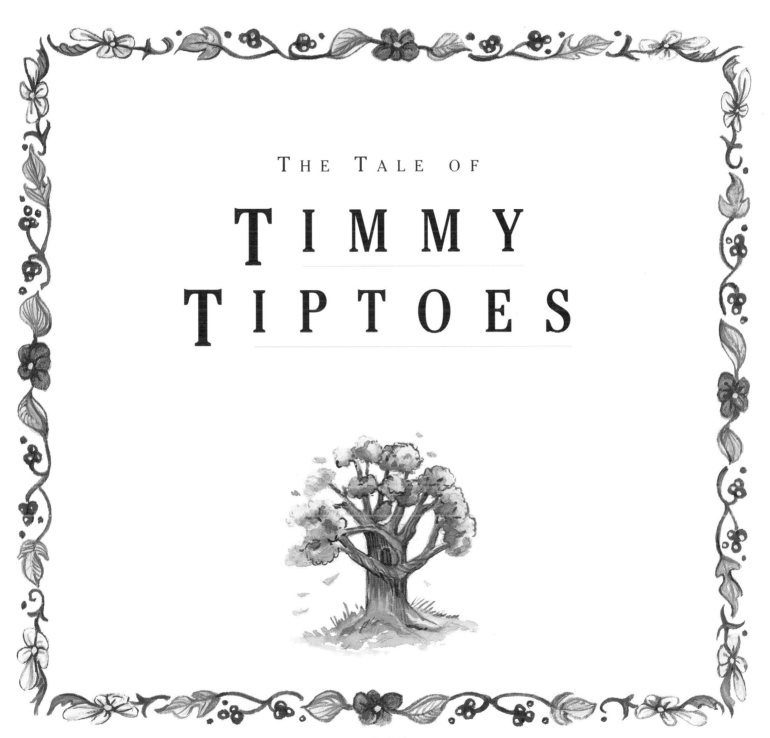

Once upon a time, there was a little fat gray squirrel named Timmy Tiptoes. He and his wife Goody lived in a nest thatched with leaves near the top of a tall tree.

"My good little wife," said the prudent Timmy one day, "we must store up some nuts for winter and spring."

And so the couple went to the nut thicket, where they found other squirrels already at work.

Timmy took off his jacket and hung it on a twig. Then he and Goody worked away quietly by themselves.

Every day they picked nuts, then carried them away in bags and stored the bags in hollow tree stumps. When the stumps were filled up, they emptied the bags into an old woodpecker hole in a hollow tree.

"How shall we ever get the nuts out again?" worried Goody.

"After sleeping through winter, my love," explained Timmy, "I shall be much thinner in spring."

Timmy and Goody were more careful than some squirrels, who often lose track of their nuts once they bury them in the ground. This was especially true of Silvertail, who was forever forgetting, then digging up someone else's nuts by mistake. This always led to a fight!

Just then, a flock of birds flew past, searching for caterpillars and spiders. The first bird sang, "Who's-been-digging-up-my-nuts? Who's-been-digging-up-my-nuts? Little-bit-o'-bread-and-no-cheese!"

The squirrels in the nut thicket followed and listened, but Timmy and Goody went on with their work. The first bird perched in a bush near them and sang his silly song again.

But the other squirrels thought it meant something very bad indeed. They jumped on Timmy, scratching and slapping him, for they thought he was a thief. Timmy turned tail and ran away.

The others caught him and dragged him up the tree with the woodpecker hole. The squirrels tried to push Timmy through the hole. But he was too plump, so they left him there, halfway in and halfway out. Somehow, Timmy wiggled through and landed on his own store of nuts. There he lay quite stunned and still.

Meanwhile, Goody had gone home. When her husband did not return, she passed an unhappy night. Next day, she went back to the thicket, but the other squirrels chased her away. So, she wandered all over the woods, calling "Timmy Tiptoes! Where, oh where is my Timmy?"

When Timmy awoke, he found himself tucked into a little moss bed. He coughed and groaned, and his ribs hurt.

A small striped chipmunk appeared holding a lamp and asked Timmy how he felt. He lent Timmy a nightcap. The house was full of food, of course, because these were the nuts Timmy had picked himself.

His host offered him some nuts—"Let me crack them for you!" he said—and soon the fat little squirrel was fatter than ever. He wondered how he would ever get out.

Goody continued to gather nuts, hiding them under a tree root. This got the attention of a little woman chipmunk.

"My husband, Chippy Hackee, has left me. What is the meaning of all these nuts?" she wanted to know.

"Beg pardon, but I didn't know anyone lived here," said Goody. "My husband, Timmy Tiptoes, has run away, too."

"I know where my husband is, for a little bird told me," said the chipmunk. She led Goody to the tree with the hole in it. They heard singing from inside—a fat squirrel voice and a thinner chipmunk voice—and the sound of nuts being cracked.

Goody thought of going in, but the chipmunk warned that Chippy Hackee might bite.

Then Goody peeped in at the hole and called to Timmy.

"Is that you, Goody Tiptoes?" her husband asked. He popped his head through the hole and kissed his wife on the snout. But he was too fat to squeeze all the way through.

Two weeks went by, and then a storm blew the top off the tree and opened up the hole. Timmy Tiptoes came out and went off with his wife under an umbrella.

Chippy Hackee stayed behind. He camped out in the wind and rain—though it was ever so uncomfortable!

At last a bear came walking through the woods. Perhaps he was looking for nuts, for he sniffed around quite a bit.

And so, Chippy Hackee decided to run for home—in a big hurry!

When the little chipmunk got home to his wife, he found he had caught a terrible head cold. He felt even worse than when he had been camping out in the tree trunk.

Timmy and Goody Tiptoes have learned an important lesson from their adventures. These days, they keep their store of nuts locked up with a little padlock.

And whenever that silly little bird sees a crowd of chipmunks or squirrels and starts singing his silly little song—"Who's-been-digging-up-my-nuts? Little-bit-o'-bread-and-no-cheese!"—

—no one with an ounce of good sense ever bothers to answer!

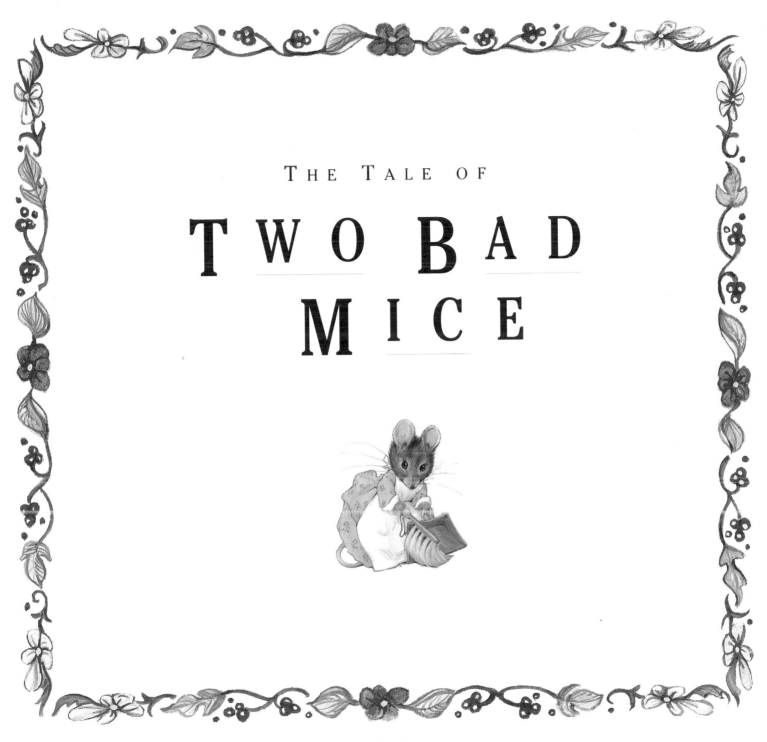

THE TALE OF

TWO BAD MICE

Once upon a time there was a very beautiful dollhouse. It was red brick with white windows, and it had real curtains, a front door, and a chimney.

It belonged to two dolls named Lucinda and Jane. It really belonged just to Lucinda; Jane was the cook. But Lucinda never asked for meals and Jane never cooked. Dinner was stored in a box, ready to eat. There were two red lobsters, a ham, a fish, pudding, and some pears and oranges. They would not come off the plates, but they were extremely beautiful.

One morning Lucinda and Jane had gone out for a ride in the doll stroller. There was no one in the nursery, and it was very quiet. Suddenly there was a little scuffling, scratching noise in a corner near the fireplace, where there was a hole in the wall.

Tom Thumb put out his head for a moment, and then popped it back in again. Tom Thumb was a mouse.

A minute later, Hunca Munca, his wife, put her head out, too. When she saw that there was no one in the nursery, she ventured out.

Tom Thumb and Hunca Munca went carefully toward the dollhouse. They pushed open the front door; it was not locked.

Tom Thumb and Hunca Munca peeked into the dining room. They squeaked with joy. Such a lovely dinner was set on the table! There were tiny spoons, knives, and forks, and two mouse-size chairs.

Tom Thumb set to work at once to carve the ham. It was plump and juicy-looking. But the knife bent and hurt him. He put his finger in his mouth.

"It is not cooked enough. It is hard. *You* try to carve it, Hunca Munca," said Tom Thumb.

Hunca Munca stood on her chair and chopped at the ham with another knife. The ham broke off the plate and rolled under the table.

"Let it alone," said Tom Thumb. "Give me some fish instead, Hunca Munca!"

Hunca Munca tried to give Tom Thumb some fish, but the fish was glued to the dish. Tom Thumb lost his temper.

He put the ham in the middle of the floor and hit it with a coal shovel—*bang, bang, smash, smash!* The ham broke into pieces. It was made of nothing but plaster and paint!

There was no end to the anger and disappointment of Tom Thumb and Hunca Munca. They smashed the pudding, the lobsters, the pears, and the oranges.

Since the fish would not come off the plate, they put it into the red paper fire in the kitchen, but it would not burn.

Tom Thumb even went up the chimney and looked out at the top, but there was no soot.

While Tom Thumb was up the chimney, Hunca Munca had yet another disappointment. She found some tiny canisters on a shelf. The canisters were labeled "Rice," "Coffee," and "Flour." But when she turned the canisters upside down, only red and blue beads spilled out!

Those two bad mice set to work to do all the mischief they could! Tom Thumb took Jane's doll clothes out of the dresser in her bedroom and threw them out the upstairs window.

Hunca Munca was not the sort to waste things, though. After she had pulled half the feathers out of Lucinda's bed pillow, Hunca Munca remembered she needed a feather bed. She and Tom Thumb carried the pillow down the stairs and into the mouse hole. It was a tight sqeeze, but they managed it somehow.

Then Hunca Munca went back to the dollhouse and took a bookcase, a bird cage, a chair, and several small odds and ends. It didn't help matters that the bookcase and the bird cage refused to go into the mouse hole.

Hunca Munca left the bookcase and bird cage next to the mouse hole and went to get a cradle. The cradle fit through the hole nicely. But just as she was returning to get another chair, there were voices outside the nursery door. The mice rushed back to their hole, and the two dolls came into the nursery.

What a sight met the eyes of Jane and Lucinda! Lucinda sat on the upset kitchen stove and stared at the mess. Jane leaned against the kitchen shelves and smiled (her face is painted in a smile). Neither of them could speak.

The little girl who owned the dollhouse said, "I will get a doll dressed like a police officer!"

The little girl's nanny said, "I will set a mousetrap!"

The bookcase and the bird cage were rescued. But Hunca Munca still has the cradle. She also has some of Lucinda's clothes and other small things.

So that is the story of the two bad mice. But they were not so very naughty after all, because Tom Thumb paid for everything he broke.

He found some money under a rug, and on Christmas Eve, he and Hunca Munca stuffed it into one of Lucinda and Jane's Christmas stockings.

And very early every morning—before anybody is awake—Hunca Munca comes with her dustpan and her broom to sweep the doll's house!

THE TALE OF
TOM KITTEN

Once there were three little kittens, and their names were Moppet, Mittens, and Tom Kitten. The kittens had beautiful little fur coats, but they liked to tumble about in the yard and play in the dust—they never stayed clean long.

One day, their mother, Mrs. Tabitha Twitchit, expected several of her fine friends for tea. She called her kittens indoors to wash and dress before her company arrived.

First, she scrubbed their faces. Next, she brushed their fur and combed their tails and whiskers. When the kittens were clean, Mrs. Tabitha dressed Moppet and Mittens in fresh dresses.

But for her son Thomas, she took all sorts of handsome—but uncomfortable!—clothes out of the dresser drawers. Tom Kitten had grown fat; three buttons popped off his jacket! His mother sewed them on again.

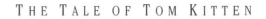

When the three kittens were ready, Mrs. Tabitha let them out to play while she made hot buttered toast for her tea party. "Now keep your clothes clean, children!" she called. "Keep away from the dirt, Sally Henny-Penny, the pig pen, and most of all, keep away from the Puddle-Ducks."

Moppet and Mittens found it difficult to walk. They tripped on the hems of their dresses and fell on their noses. When they stood up, there were several green stains.

"Let's climb up the rocks, and sit on the garden wall," said Moppet. They turned their dresses back to front, and scampered up onto the wall.

Tom Kitten could not jump while wearing trousers. He slowly climbed the rocks, holding onto ferns. He popped buttons right and left! He was in pieces by the time he reached the top of the garden wall.

Moppet and Mittens tried to pull him together, but his hat fell off, and the rest of his buttons burst. Tom wriggled out of his little coat and trousers. They landed in a heap on the ground.

In the middle of all this trouble, the kittens heard a *pit pat paddle pat!* The three Puddle-Ducks were coming down the road. They were marching one behind the other and doing the goose step, *pit pat paddle pat! pit pat waddle pat!*

The Puddle-Ducks stopped and stood in a row and stared up at the kittens. They had very small eyes, and they looked surprised.

Then, Rebecca and Jemima Puddle-Duck picked up Tom's hat and Moppet's lace handkerchief and put them on!

Mr. Drake Puddle-Duck thought this looked like a good idea. He picked up Tom's suit and put it on himself! "It's a fine morning!" he quacked. The suit fit Mr. Drake even worse than it fit Tom Kitten.

Moppet, Mittens, and Tom Kitten laughed so hard they nearly fell off the wall!

Mr. Drake, Rebecca, and Jemima Puddle-Duck waddled up the road with a *pit pat paddle pat, pit pat waddle pat.* They were a sight!

Mrs. Tabitha Twitchit came down the garden walk and found her kittens wearing none of their fine clothes. She scolded them and dragged them back to the house.

"My friends will arrive in a minute, and you are not fit to be seen. I am embarrassed!" said Mrs. Tabitha Twitchit.

Moppet, Mittens, and Tom were sent up to their room. When her friends arrived, Mrs. Tabitha told them that her little kittens were in bed sick with the measles (which, of course, was not true at all).

Oh, no! Those three little kittens were not in bed, *not* in the least. Mrs. Tabitha Twitchit's guests heard some *very* strange noises coming from upstairs. The ladies found their quiet tea party to be spoiled.

I think that some day I shall have to write another— longer—book to tell you more about Tom Kitten!

And as for the Puddle-Ducks, who went into a pond, their clothes all came off, for there were no buttons left to hold them on. Mr. Drake, Rebecca, and Jemima Puddle-Duck have been looking for their fine clothes ever since!